RETURN THIS BOOK TO:

MY MOM TRAVELS A LOT

MY MOM TRAVELS A LOT

by
CAROLINE FELLER BAUER
Illustrated by
NANCY WINSLOW PARKER

PUFFIN BOOKS

PUFFIN BOOKS
Published by the Penguin Group, Penguin Books USA Inc.,
375 Hudson Street, New York, New York 10014, U.S.A.
Penguin Books Ltd, 27 Wrights Lane, London W8 5TZ, England
Penguin Books Australia Ltd, Ringwood, Victoria, Australia
Penguin Books Canada Ltd, 10 Alcorn Avenue, Toronto, Ontario, Canada M4V 3B2
Penguin Books (N.Z.) Ltd, 182–190 Wairau Road, Auckland, 10, New Zealand

Penguin Books Ltd, Registered Offices: Harmondsworth, Middlesex, England

First published by Frederick Warne & Co., Inc., 1981
Published in Picture Puffins 1985
7   9   10   8

Library of Congress Cataloging in Publication Data
Bauer, Caroline Feller.   My mom travels a lot.
Summary: A child points out the good and bad things about a mother's job that takes her from home a lot.
1. Children's stories, American.   [1. Mothers—
Employment—Fiction]   I. Parker, Nancy Winslow, ill.   II. Title.
[PZ7.B3258My   1985]   [E]   84-22262   ISBN 0-14-050545-8

Printed in U.S.A.
Set in Memphis Medium Condensed

To
HILARY,
the best

MY MOM TRAVELS A LOT

My mom travels a lot.

The good thing about it is
we get to go to the airport.

The bad thing about it is
there's only one nighttime kiss.

The bad thing about it is
Mom wasn't home when Susie
had her puppies.

The good thing about it is
we get lots of postcards.

The bad
thing
about it is
Mom
missed
the school
play.

The good thing about it is
Dad and I eat out more often.

The bad thing about it is
I always forget to water
the plants.

The good thing about it is
I don't always have to make
my bed.

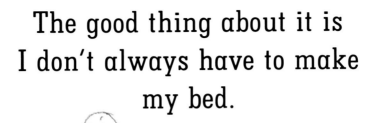

The bad thing about it is
Dad can never find my boots.

The good thing about it is
sometimes I get to stay
up late.

The bad thing about it is
we miss her.

The good thing about it is
we get presents.

But the best thing about it is

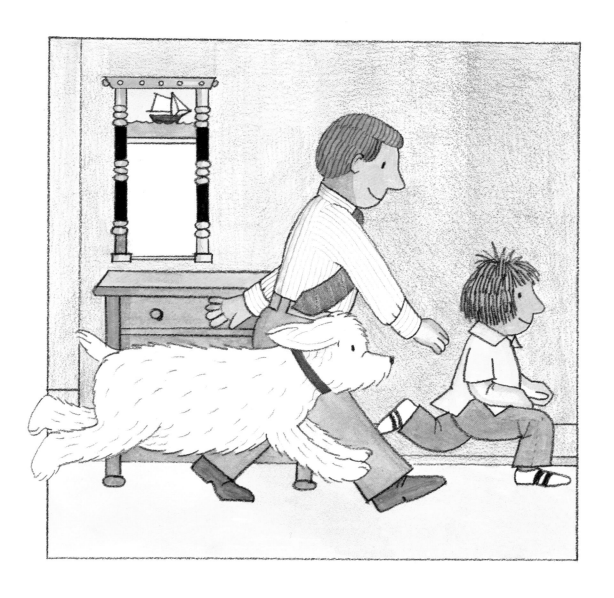

she always comes back!

The end.

CAROLINE FELLER BAUER has lectured on children's books in the United States and Canada, as well as in Saudi Arabia, Australia, and Singapore. Dr. Bauer, who earned an M.A. in library science from Columbia University, in New York, and a Ph.D. in communications from the University of Oregon, lives in Portland, Oregon, with her husband, Peter, their daughter, Hilary, and a Bedlington terrier named Robbie. Dr. Bauer has her own storytelling program on local television called Caroline's Corner.

NANCY WINSLOW PARKER always wanted to be a children's book author and illustrator. She studied fine arts at Mills College in California and worked in publishing and media before her first book was accepted for publication in 1974. Ms. Parker divides her time between Mantoloking, New Jersey, and New York City.